RAINBOW magic

RAINBOW FAIRIES

AMBER
THE ORANGE FAIRY

By Daisy Meadows
Illustrated by Georgie Ripper

Silver Dolphin

Silver Dolphin

Silver Dolphin Books
An imprint of Printers Row Publishing Group
A division of Readerlink Distribution Services, LLC
9717 Pacific Heights Blvd, San Diego, CA 92121
www.silverdolphinbooks.com

Printers Row Publishing Group is a division of
Readerlink Distribution Services, LLC.
Silver Dolphin Books is a registered trademark of
Readerlink Distribution Services, LLC.

All notations of errors or omissions should be addressed to Silver
Dolphin Books, Editorial Department, at the above address. All other
correspondence (author inquiries, permissions) concerning the
content of this book should be addressed to:
Hachette Children's Group
Carmelite House
50 Victoria Embankment
London
EC4Y 0DZ

ISBN: 978-1-6672-0435-2
Manufactured, printed, and assembled in Pittston, PA, USA.
First printing, February 2023. KA/02/23
27 26 25 24 23   1 2 3 4 5

AMBER
THE ORANGE FAIRY

The
Fairyland
Palace

Maze

Forest

Orchard

Black
Pot

Meadow

Tower

Beach

Tide pools

Rainspell Island

Jack Frost's Ice Castle

Tom Goodfellow's House

Merry-go-round

Willow Tree

Mrs. Merry's Cottage

Stream

Field

Town

Mermaid Cottage

Harbor

Dolphin Cottage

Cold winds blow and thick ice form,
I conjure up this fairy storm.
To seven corners of the human world
the Rainbow Fairies will be hurled!

I curse every part of Fairyland,
with a frosty wave of my icy hand.
For now and always, from this day,
Fairyland will be cold and gray!

Ruby is safely hidden in the pot at the end of the rainbow. Now Rachel and Kirsty must find **Amber the Orange Fairy**.

Table of Contents

A Very Unusual
SHELL

"What a beautiful day!" Rachel Walker shouted, staring up at the blue sky. She and her friend Kirsty Tate were running along Rainspell Island's yellow, sandy beach. Their parents walked a little way behind them.

"It's a *magical* day," Kirsty added. The two friends smiled at each other.

Rachel and Kirsty had come to
Rainspell Island for their vacations.
But they soon found out it really *was* a
magical place!

As they ran, they passed tide pools that
sparkled like jewels in the sunshine.

Rachel spotted a little *splash!* in one of
the pools. "There's something in there,
Kirsty!" She pointed. "Let's go look."

The girls jogged over to the pool and
crouched down to see.

Kirsty's heart thumped as she gazed into the crystal-clear water. "What is it?" she asked.

Suddenly, the water rippled. A little brown crab scuttled sideways across the sandy bottom and disappeared under a rock.

Kirsty felt disappointed. "I thought it might be another Rainbow Fairy," she said.

"So did I." Rachel sighed. "Never mind. We'll keep looking."

"Of course we will," Kirsty agreed. Then she put her finger to her lips as their parents came up behind them. "*Shhh.*"

Kirsty and Rachel had a big secret. They were helping to find the seven missing Rainbow Fairies. Jack Frost put a wicked spell on the fairies and trapped them on Rainspell Island. The Rainbow Fairies made Fairyland bright and colorful. Until they were all found, Fairyland would be dark and gray.

Rachel looked at the shimmering blue sea. "Do you want to go swimming?" she asked.

But Kirsty wasn't listening. She was shading her eyes with her hand and looking farther along the beach. "Look over there, Rachel—by those rocks," she said.

Then Rachel could see it too—something glittering and sparkling in the sunshine. "Wait for me!" she called, as Kirsty hurried down the beach.

When they saw what it was, the two friends sighed in disappointment.

"It's just the wrapper from a chocolate bar," Rachel said sadly. She bent down and picked up the shiny purple foil.

Kirsty thought for a moment. "Do you remember what the Fairy Queen told us?" she asked.

Rachel nodded. "*Let the magic come to you,*" she said. "You're right, Kirsty. We should just enjoy our vacation, and wait for the magic to happen. After all, that's how we found Ruby in the pot at the end of the rainbow, isn't it?" She put her beach bag down on the sand. "Come on—race you into the water!"

They rushed into the water. The sea was cold and salty, but the sun felt warm on their backs. They waved at their parents, sitting on the sand, and splashed around in the waves until they got goose bumps.

"Ow!" Kirsty gasped as they paddled out of the water. "I just stepped on something sharp."

"It might have been a shell," said Rachel. "There are lots of them around here." She picked up a pale pink one and showed it to Kirsty.

"Let's see how many we can find," Kirsty said.

The two girls walked along the beach looking for shells. They found long, thin, blue shells and tiny, round, white shells.

Soon their hands were full.
They had walked right
around the curve of
the bay.
Rachel looked over
her shoulder and a
sudden gust of wind
whipped her hair
across her face.
"Look how far
we've come," she
said. Kirsty stopped.
The wind blew at
her back and made
goose bumps stand
out on her arms.
"It's getting cold
now," she said.
"Should we go back?"

"Yes, it must be almost lunchtime," said Rachel.

The two girls began to walk back along the beach. They'd only gone a few steps when the wind suddenly stopped.

"That's funny," said Kirsty. "It's not windy here at all."

They looked back and saw perfect little swirls of sand being lifted by the wind. "Oh!" said Rachel, and the two friends looked at each other in excitement.

"It's magic," Kirsty whispered. "It just *has* to be!"

They walked back to where they had
been, and the breeze swirled around their
legs again. Then the golden sand at their
feet began to drift gently to one side, as
if invisible hands were pushing it away.
A large scallop shell appeared. It was
much bigger than the other shells on the
beach. It was a light peach color with soft
orange streaks, and it was tightly closed.

Quickly the girls kneeled down on the sand, dropping the little shells from their hands. Kirsty was just about to pick up the scallop shell when Rachel put out her hand. "Listen," she whispered.

They both listened hard.

Rachel smiled when she heard the sound again.

Inside the shell, a tiny voice hummed softly . . .

THE MAGIC FEATHER

Very carefully, Rachel picked up the shell. It felt warm and smooth. *Hummm...*

The humming stopped at once. "I should not be scared," said the tiny voice. "I just have to be brave, and help will come very soon."

Kirsty put her face close to the shell. "Hello," she whispered. "Is there a fairy in there?"

"Yes!" cried the voice. "I'm Amber the Orange Fairy! Can you get me out of here?"

"Of course we will," Kirsty promised. "My name is Kirsty, and my friend Rachel is here, too." She looked up at Rachel, her eyes shining. "We've found another Rainbow Fairy!"

"Quick," Rachel said. "Let's get the shell open." She took hold of the scallop shell and tried to pull the two halves apart. Nothing happened.

"Try again," said
Kirsty. She and Rachel
each grasped one half
of the shell and tugged.
But the shell stayed
tightly shut.

"What's happening?"
Amber called. She sounded worried.

"We can't open the shell," Kirsty said.
"But we'll think of something." She
turned to Rachel. "If we find a piece of
driftwood, maybe we could use it to
open the shell."

Rachel glanced around the beach.
"I don't see any driftwood," she said.
"We could try tapping the shell
on a rock."

"But that might hurt Amber," Kirsty
pointed out.

Suddenly, Rachel remembered
something. "What about the magic bags
the Fairy Queen gave us?" she said.

"Of course!" Kirsty cried. She put her
face close to the shell again.
"Amber, we're going to
look in our magic
bags," she said.
"OK, but please
hurry," Amber called.
Rachel opened her
beach bag. The two
magic bags were hidden
under her towel. One of the bags
was glowing with a golden light.
Carefully, Rachel pulled it out.

"Look," she whispered to Kirsty. "This
one is all lit up."

"Open it, quick," Kirsty whispered back.

As Rachel undid the bag, a fountain
of glittering sparks flew out.

"What's inside?" Kirsty asked, gently
putting down the shell.

Rachel slid her hand into the bag.
She could feel something light and soft.
She pulled it out, scattering sparkles
everywhere. It was a shimmering
golden feather.

Kirsty and Rachel stared at the feather. "It's really pretty," said Kirsty. "But what are we going to *do* with it?"

"I don't know," Rachel replied. She tried to use the feather to push the two halves of the shell apart. But the feather just curled up in her hand. "Maybe we should ask Amber."

"Amber, we've looked in the magic bags," Kirsty said, "and we've found a feather."

"Oh, good!" Amber said happily from inside the shell. "That's wonderful news!"

"But we don't know what to do with it," Rachel added.

Amber laughed. It sounded like the tinkle of a tiny bell. "You tickle the shell, of course!" she said.

"Do you think that will work?" Rachel said to Kirsty.

"Let's give it a try," Kirsty said.

Rachel began to tickle the shell with the feather. At first nothing happened. Then they heard a soft, gritty chuckle, followed by a tinkly giggle from inside the shell. Then another chuckle, and another. Slowly, the two halves of the shell began to open.

"It's working," Kirsty gasped. "Keep tickling, Rachel!"

The shell was laughing hard now. The two halves opened wider . . .

And there, sitting inside the smooth, peach-colored shell, was Amber the Orange Fairy.

A STRANGER IN THE POT

"I'm free!" Amber cried joyfully.

She shot out of the shell and up into the air, her wings fluttering in a rainbow-colored blur. Orange fairy dust floated down around Kirsty and Rachel. It turned into orange bubbles as it fell. One of the bubbles landed on Rachel's arm and burst with a tiny *pop*!

"The bubbles smell like oranges!" Rachel said with a smile.

Amber spun through the sky, turning cartwheels one after the other. "Thank you!" she called. Then she swooped down toward Rachel and Kirsty.

She wore a shiny orange leotard and tall boots. Her brown hair was held in a high ponytail, tied with a band of peach blossoms. In her hand was an orange wand tipped with gold.

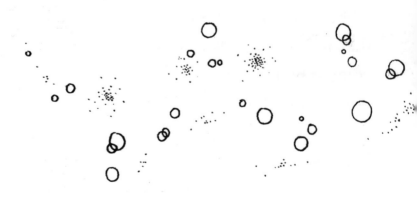

"I'm so glad you found me!" Amber shouted. She landed on Rachel's shoulder, then cartwheeled lightly across to Kirsty's. "But who are you? And where are my Rainbow sisters? And what's happening in Fairyland? How am I going to get back there?"

She was talking so fast that Kirsty and Rachel couldn't get a word in.

Suddenly, Amber stopped. She floated down and landed softly on Rachel's hand. "I'm sorry," she said with a smile. "But I haven't had anyone to talk to. I've been shut up in that shell ever since Jack Frost's spell banished us from Fairyland. How did you know where to find me?"

"Kirsty and I promised your sister Ruby that we would look for all the Rainbow Fairies," Rachel told her.

"Ruby?" Amber's face lit up. She spun around on Rachel's hand. "You've found Ruby?"

"Yes, she's safe now," Rachel said. "She's in the pot at the end of the rainbow."

Amber did a happy backflip. "Please take me to her!" she begged.

"I'll ask our parents if we can go for a walk," Kirsty said. And she ran off across the beach.

"Do you know what is
happening in Fairyland?"
Amber asked Rachel.

Rachel nodded.
She and Kirsty had
flown with Ruby to
Fairyland. Ruby had
used her wand to
shrink them to fairy
size, and she had
given them magical
fairy wings. "King
Oberon and Queen
Titania miss you
very much," Rachel
told Amber. "With
no color, Fairyland
is a sad place."

Kirsty was hurrying back toward them. "Mom said we can go for a walk," she panted.

"Well, what are we waiting for? Let's go!" Amber called. She flew up and did a somersault in midair.

Rachel pulled their shorts, T-shirts, and sneakers out of her beach bag and both girls put them on.

"Rachel, could you bring my shell?" Amber asked. Rachel looked surprised.

"Yes, if you want," she said. Amber nodded. "It's really comfy," she explained. "It will make a nice bed for me and my sisters."

Rachel put the shell in her beach bag and they set off with Amber sitting cross-legged on Kirsty's shoulder.

"My wings are a bit stiff after being in the shell," she told them. "I don't think I can fly very far yet."

The girls followed the path to the clearing in the woods where the pot at the end of the rainbow was hidden.

"Here we are," said Rachel. "The pot is right over there." She stopped. The pot was where they'd left it—under the weeping willow tree. But climbing out of it was a big, green frog.

"Oh no!" Rachel gasped. She and Kirsty stared at the frog in horror. Where was Ruby?

HOME SWEET HOME

Rachel dashed forward and grabbed the frog around his plump, green belly.

The frog turned his head and glared at her, his eyes bulging. "And what do you think *you're* doing?" he croaked.

Rachel was so shocked, she let go of the frog. He hopped away from her, looking very annoyed.

"It's a talking frog!" Kirsty gasped, her eyes wide. "And it looks like it's wearing glasses . . ."

"Bertram!" Amber flew down from Kirsty's shoulder. "I didn't know it was you."

Bertram bowed his head as Amber hugged him. "Thank goodness you're safe, Miss Amber!" he said happily. "And may I say, it's very good to see you again."

Amber beamed at Rachel and Kirsty. "Bertram isn't an ordinary frog, you know," she explained. "He's one of King Oberon's footmen. He works closely with the king and queen."

"Oh, yes!" said Kirsty. "I remember now. We saw the frog footmen when we went to Fairyland with Ruby."

"But they were wearing uniforms then," Rachel added.

"Excuse me, Miss, but a frog in a uniform would *not* be a good idea on Rainspell Island," Bertram pointed out. "It's much better if I look like an ordinary frog."

"But what are you doing here, Bertram?" asked Amber. "And where's Ruby?"

"Don't worry, Miss Amber," Bertram replied. "Miss Ruby is safe in the pot." He suddenly looked very stern. "King Oberon sent me to Rainspell. The Cloud Fairies spotted Jack Frost's goblins sneaking out of Fairyland. We think he has sent them here to stop you from finding the Rainbow Fairies."

Kirsty felt a shiver run down her spine. "Jack Frost's goblins?" she said.

"They're his servants," Amber explained. Her wings trembled and she looked very scared. "They want to keep Fairyland cold and gray!"

"Never fear, Miss Amber," Bertram croaked. "I'm here to look after you and keep the Rainbow Fairies safe."

Suddenly, a shower of red fairy dust shot out of the pot. Ruby fluttered out. "I heard voices," she shouted joyfully. "Amber! I *knew* it was you!"

"Ruby!" Amber called. And then she cartwheeled through the air toward her sister.

Rachel and Kirsty watched as the two fairies flew into each other's arms. The air around them fizzed with little red flowers and orange bubbles.

"Thank you, Kirsty and Rachel," said
Ruby. She and Amber floated down to
them, holding hands. "It's so good to
have Amber back safely."

"What about you?"
Rachel asked. "Have you
been OK in the pot?"

Ruby nodded. "I'm
fine now that Bertram is
here," she replied. "And
I've been making the pot into
a fairy home. We can stay there until all
our fairy sisters are found."

"I brought my shell with me," Amber
said. "It will make a nice bed for us.
Could you show her, Rachel?"

Rachel put her bag down on the
grass and took the peach-colored shell
out of it.

"It's beautiful," said Ruby. Then she smiled at Rachel and Kirsty. "Would you like to come and see our new home?" she asked.

"But the pot's too small for Kirsty and me to fit inside," Rachel began. Then she began to tingle with excitement. "Oh! Are you going to make us fairy size again?"

Ruby nodded. She and Amber flew over the girls' heads, showering them with fairy dust. Rachel and Kirsty started to shrink, just as they had before. Soon they were the same size as Ruby and Amber.

"I *love* being a fairy," Kirsty said
happily. She twisted around to look
at her silvery wings.

"Me too," Rachel agreed. She was
getting used to seeing flowers as tall
as trees!

Bertram hopped over to the pot. "I'll
wait outside," he croaked.

"Come this way,"
said Ruby. She took
Rachel's hand, and
Amber took Kirsty's.
Then the fairies led
them toward the pot.

Rachel and Kirsty
fluttered through the air,
dodging a butterfly that was as
big as they were. Its wings felt like velvet
as they brushed gently past it.

"I'm getting better at flying!" Kirsty laughed as she landed neatly on the edge of the pot. She looked down eagerly.

The pot was full of sunlight. There were little chairs made from twigs tied with blades of grass. Each chair had a cushion made from a soft red berry. Rugs of bright green leaves covered the floor.

"Should we bring in the shell?" asked Rachel.

The others thought this was a very good idea. When they flew out of the pot, Bertram was already pushing the shell across the grass toward them.

"Here you are," he croaked.

The shell seemed very heavy now that Rachel and Kirsty were the same size as Ruby and Amber. But Bertram helped them to lift it into the pot.

Soon the shell bed sat neatly inside. Ruby lined it with sweet-smelling rose petals.

"The pot looks beautiful," Rachel said.

"I wish I could live here, too!" said Kirsty.

Ruby turned to her sister. "Do you like it, Amber?" she asked.

"It's beautiful," Amber replied. "It reminds me of our house back in Fairyland. I wish I could see Fairyland again. I miss it so much."

Ruby smiled. "Well, we can't go back to Fairyland for good until we're all together," she explained. "But I can *show* you Fairyland. Follow me!"

Bertram was still on guard next to the pot when they flew outside again. "Where are you going, Miss Ruby?" he croaked.

"To the magic pond," Ruby replied. "Come with us." She sprinkled her magic dust over Rachel and Kirsty. Quickly, they grew back to their normal size.

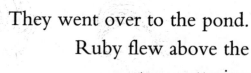

They went over to the pond. Ruby flew above the water, scattering fairy dust. Just like before, a picture began to appear. "Fairyland!" Amber cried, gazing into the water. Rachel and Kirsty watched too. Fairyland still looked sad and chilly. The palace, the toadstool houses, flowers, and the trees were all icy and gray.

Suddenly, a cold breeze rippled the surface of the water, and the picture began to fade.

"What's happening?" Kirsty whispered.

Everyone stared down at the pond.

Another picture was taking shape—a
thin, grinning face with frosty white hair,
and icicles hanging from his beard.

"Jack Frost!" Ruby gasped in horror.
As she spoke, the air turned icy cold and
the edges of the pool began to freeze.

"What's happening?" Rachel asked, shivering.

Bertram hopped forward. "This is bad news," he said. "It means that Jack Frost's goblins must be close by!"

GOBLIN ALERT!

Rachel and Kirsty felt shivers run down their spines as the whole pond froze over. Jack Frost's grinning face faded away.

"Follow me," ordered Bertram. He hopped over to a large bush. "We'll hide here."

"Maybe we should go back to the pot," said Ruby.

"Not if the goblins are close by," Bertram replied. "We can't let them know where the pot is."

The two girls crouched behind the bush next to Bertram. Ruby and Amber sat very still on Kirsty's shoulder. It was getting colder and colder. Rachel and Kirsty couldn't stop their teeth from chattering.

"What are the goblins like?" Rachel asked.

"They're bigger than we are," said Amber. She was trembling with fright.

"And they have mean faces and long noses and big feet," Ruby added, holding her sister's hand for comfort.

"Hush, Miss Ruby," Bertram croaked. "I can hear something."

Rachel and Kirsty listened. Suddenly, Rachel saw a long-nosed shadow dash across the clearing toward them. She grabbed Kirsty's arm. They were peering out of the bush when the leaves rustled right next to them. They almost jumped out of their skin.

"Hey!" said a gruff voice, sounding very close. "What do you think you're doing?"

Rachel and Kirsty held their breath.

"Nothing," said another gruff voice.

"Goblins!" Amber whispered in Kirsty's ear.

"You stepped on my toe," said the first goblin angrily.

"No, I didn't," snapped the other goblin.

"Yes, you did! Keep your big feet to yourself!"

"Well, at least my nose isn't as big as yours!"

The bush shook. It sounded as if the goblins were pushing and shoving each other.

"Get out of my way!" one of them shouted. "Ow!"

"That'll teach you to push *me*!" yelled the other one.

Rachel and Kirsty looked at each other in alarm. What if the goblins found them there?

"Come on," puffed one of the goblins. "Jack Frost will be really angry if we don't find these fairies. You know he wants us to keep them from getting back to Fairyland."

"Well, they're not here, are they?" grumbled the other. "Let's try somewhere else."

The voices died away. The leaves stopped rustling. Suddenly, the air felt warm again. There was a cracking sound as the frozen pond began to melt.

"They're gone," Bertram croaked. "Quick, we must get back to the pot."

They all hurried across the clearing. The pot stood under the weeping willow tree, just as before.

"I'll stay outside in case the goblins come back," Bertram began. But a shout from Kirsty stopped them all in their tracks.

"Look!" she cried. "The pot's frozen over!"

Kirsty was right. The top of the pot was covered with a thick sheet of ice. No one, not even a fairy, could get inside.

BERTRAM TO THE RESCUE

"Oh no!" Ruby gasped. "The goblins must have been really close. Thank goodness they didn't discover the pot."

She flew over to the pot with Amber right behind her. They drummed on the ice with their tiny fists. But it was too thick for them to break through.

"Should *we* try, Rachel?" asked Kirsty. "Maybe we could smash the ice with a stick."

But Bertram had another idea. "Stand back, please, everyone," he said.

The girls moved to the edge of the clearing. Ruby sat on Kirsty's hand, and Amber flew over to Rachel. They all watched.

Suddenly, Bertram leaped forward with a mighty hop. He jumped straight at the sheet of ice, kicking out with his webbed feet. But the ice did not break. "Let's try again," he panted.

He jumped forward again and hit the ice. This time, there was a loud cracking sound. After one more jump, the ice shattered into little pieces. Some of it fell inside the pot. Rachel and Kirsty rushed over to fish out the pieces of ice before they melted.

"There you are," Bertram croaked.

"Thank you, Bertram," Ruby called. She and Amber flew down and hugged the frog.

Bertram looked pleased. "Just doing my job, Miss Ruby," he said. "You and Miss Amber must stay very close to the pot from now on. It's dangerous for you to go too far."

"We have to say good-
bye to our friends first,"
Amber told him. She flew
into the air and did a
backflip, smiling at Rachel
and Kirsty. "Thank you a
thousand times."

"We'll see you again soon,"
said Rachel.

"When we've found your next
Rainbow sister," Kirsty added.

"Good luck!" said Ruby. "We'll be
waiting here for you. Come on, Amber."

She took her sister's hand, and
they flew over to the pot.
The two fairies turned to
wave at the girls. Then they
disappeared inside.

"Don't worry," Bertram said. "I'll look after them."

"We know you will," Rachel said, as she picked up her beach bag. She and Kirsty walked out of the woods. "I'm glad Ruby isn't on her own anymore," said Rachel. "Now she has Amber *and* Bertram."

"I didn't like those goblins," Kirsty said with a shudder. "I hope they don't come back again."

The girls made their way back to the beach. Their parents were packing up their towels. Rachel's dad saw Rachel and Kirsty coming down the path and went to meet them. "You've been gone a long time," he smiled. "We were just coming to look for you."

"Are we going back to the cottage now?" Rachel asked.

Mr. Walker nodded. "It's very strange," he said. "It's suddenly turned quite chilly."

As he spoke, a cold breeze swirled around Rachel and Kirsty. They shivered and looked up at the sky. The sun had disappeared behind a thick, black cloud. The trees swayed in the wind, and the leaves rustled as if they were whispering to one another.

"Jack Frost's goblins are still here!" Kirsty gasped.

"You're right," Rachel agreed. "Let's hope Bertram can keep Ruby and Amber safe while we look for the other Rainbow Fairies."

Kirsty nodded and smiled at Rachel. They still had five fairies to find. It would take some magic and a lot of work, but she was sure they could do it together!

Now it's time for Kirsty and
Rachel to help . . .

SUNNY the YELLOW FAIRY.

Read on for a sneak peek . . .

A VERY BIG BEE

"Over here, Kirsty!" called Rachel
Walker. Kirsty Tate ran across one of the
emerald-green fields that covered this part
of Rainspell Island. Buttercups and daisies
dotted the grass.

"Don't go too far!" Kirsty's mom called.
She and Kirsty's dad were climbing over a
fence at the top of the field.

Kirsty caught up with her friend.
"What did you find, Rachel? Is it another
Rainbow Fairy?" she asked hopefully.

"I don't know." Rachel was standing
on the bank of a rippling stream. "I
thought I heard something."

Kirsty's face lit up. "Maybe there's a
fairy in the stream?"

Rachel nodded. She knelt down on
the soft grass and put her ear close to
the water.

Kirsty crouched down too, and
listened really hard.

The sun glittered on the water as it
splashed over big, shiny pebbles. Tiny
rainbows flashed and sparkled—red,
orange, yellow, green, blue, indigo,
and violet.

And then the girls heard a tiny bubbling voice. "Follow me . . ." it gurgled. "Follow me . . ."

"Oh!" Rachel gasped. "Did you hear that?"

"Yes," said Kirsty, her eyes wide. "It must be a *magic* stream!"

Rachel's heart beat fast. "Maybe the stream will lead us to the Yellow Fairy," she said.

RAINBOW magic

More Titles to Read

RAINBOW FAIRIES:
RUBY THE RED FAIRY

RAINBOW FAIRIES:
SUNNY THE YELLOW FAIRY

RAINBOW FAIRIES:
FERN THE GREEN FAIRY

RAINBOW FAIRIES:
SKY THE BLUE FAIRY

RAINBOW FAIRIES:
INKY THE INDIGO FAIRY

RAINBOW FAIRIES:
HEATHER THE VIOLET FAIRY

☆ ☆ ☆ ☆ ☆ ☆ ☆

BEHIND THE MAGIC

DAISY MEADOWS is a pseudonym for the four writers of the internationally best-selling *Rainbow Magic* series: Narinder Dhami, Sue Bentley, Linda Chapman, and Sue Mongredien. *Rainbow Magic* is the no.1 bestselling series for children ages 5 and up with over 40 million copies sold worldwide!

GEORGIE RIPPER was born in London and is a children's book illustrator known for her work on the *Rainbow Magic* series of fairy books. She won the Macmillan Prize for Picture Book Illustration in 2000 with *My Best Friend Bob* and *Little Brown Bushrat*, which she wrote and illustrated.